To Christina

Dedicated to anyone who feels that they don't fit in

Marion Shardell

The Incredible Creatures of the Secret Ark

Written by Marion Sharville
Illustrated by Tim Sharville

At the time of the Great Flood, Noah sailed away on his ark, unaware that he had left behind a group of animals. They had lived deep in the forest, preferring to keep themselves to themselves.

Their leader was a gubbem, the only animal who could read and write and draw on cave walls. Hearing on Pigeon Airways that a flood was imminent, he and the other creatures watched Noah building his Ark. Gubbem decided that they could make one of their own.

At night they snuck into Noah's boatyard for oddments of timber. By the time the first drops of rain fell, they too had their own ark, and as the waters rose the crazy little craft sailed forth.

One night, the paths of the two vessels crossed and Noah, shocked at seeing another ark, stood scratching his head in utter bewilderment, muttering, "I thought mine was the only one…"

As self-proclaimed captain, Gubbem made a passenger list, naming them all in alphabetical order, keeping G for himself.

Feeling creative, he also added a verse and a drawing of each one. He put the list in a bottle and threw it overboard, hoping that one day it would be found and kept for posterity.

It has been,
and here it is.

A

The **Aristo Beast** sits covered in yeast,
in a warm place in front of the fire.
It's of lowly descent but is certain it's meant
that it should rise higher and higher.

The **Bogley Toad**, with big webbed feet, is quite impervious to heat.
Boiled or fried or simply stewed, the Bogley Toad is never rude.
But in cold weather he's ferocious, and his language is atrocious.

B

C

The **Co-Agula** lives on clotted cream
and has a large proboscis.
Its diet never varies,
and they all die from thrombosis.

The **Dribbling Cahoot** makes its home in a boot;
left or right, black or brown it won't matter.
It sits and makes faces through the holes for the laces;
of course it's as mad as a hatter.

D

E

The **Ectophant** pours out its love song in the key of F.
It's a waste of a beautiful melody
because its mate is stone deaf.

The **Felpworm** tunnels underground,
striving for its goal;
searching, ever searching
to find a better hole.

If, in its quest, it does succeed
and its efforts are not in vain,
it will spend its days in complete content,
asleep in a council drain.

F

The **Gubbem** is very intelligent and has even learned to read,
but the shortage of reading matter is very acute indeed.
For it lives far away with its family,
with whom it can hardly cope, an'
by the time it gets to the library it's hardly ever open.

G

The **Halibeak** lives on rotting weeds,
to be found in green slimy rivers.
They may look cute and cuddly to you
but they have disgusting livers.

H

I

The **Igonou** is a dear little pet;
it is small and furry and round.
You may have a job to feed it though;
it eats elephant meat by the pound.

The **Janopig** eats
its food with a spade,
but always insists
that the table is laid.

J

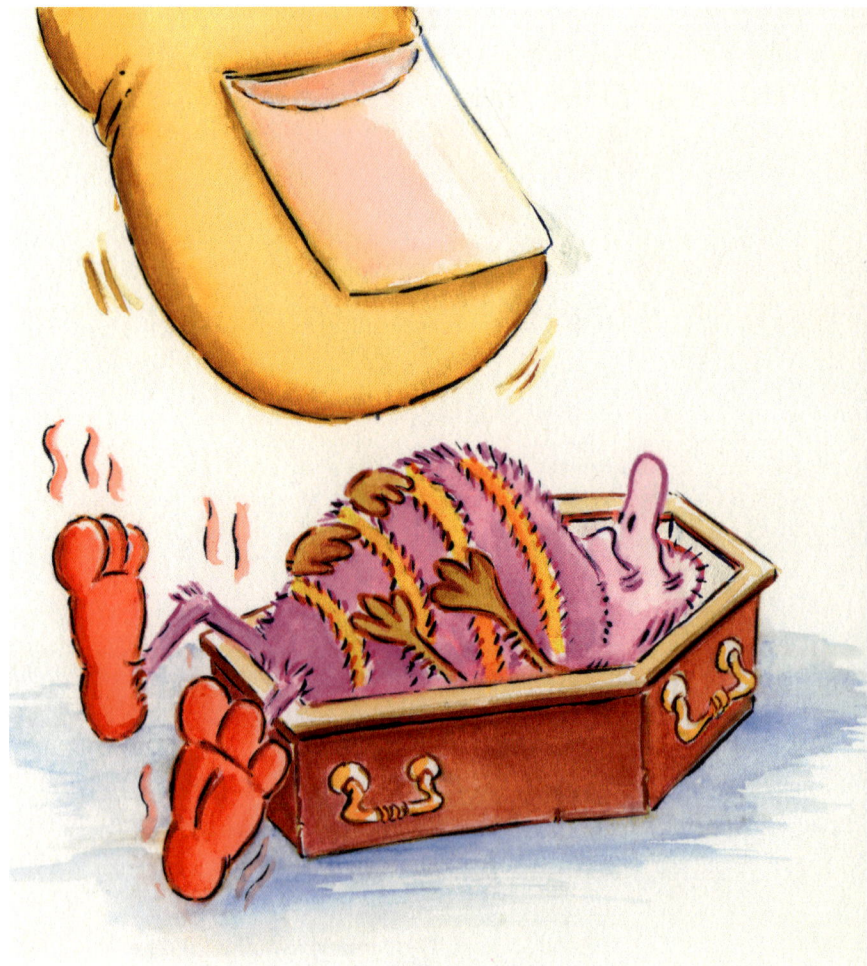

The **Konipa Flea**
lives to seventy-three
and hops all that time,
quite unwillingly.

When the time
comes to die,
it says with a sigh,
"Thank goodness,
my feet are killing me."

K

The **Lumpana** has thousands of tiny legs,
and keeps on running about.
But the back ones run faster than the front
and it ends up inside out.

L

M

The **Mockle Fly** has fifty-two wings
but cannot get off the ground,
for it's only a couple of inches long
and each wing weighs over a pound.

The **Night Creek** is an elegant bird
with a manner very imposing.
It makes its nest in a greengrocer's shop,
and mates only on early closing.

N

O

The **Orbitus** shoots straight up in the air
whenever it hears a noise.
Its nerves are in a terrible state
and I fear it's allergic to boys.

The **Paw-Sepaws** live confusing lives,
for each of them has several wives.
They do not suffer from frustrations,
only from their Paw relations.

P

The **Query Bird** calls, "Who am I?"
for him it's the burning question.
For he always loses his memory,
whenever he gets indigestion.

Q

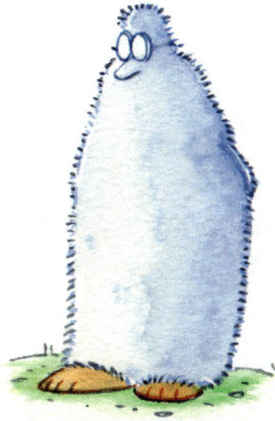

The **Rarebit** lives all its life in a hole,
with its hands behind it, linked.
It never sees another soul,
and the breed is now extinct.

GO AWAY

NOBODY LIVES HERE

R

The **Soporific Snake**
finds it hard to keep awake
while slithering along the top-most branches.
But its view of life is such,
nothing matters very much,
so it shuts its eyes, content to take its chances.

S

The **Tortle-Frog**
from the Himalayas
always wears pyjamas.
It looks a pet
in its flannelette,
and amuses all the lamas.

T

The **Umbilicus** is a shy little thing,
and will not answer your call.
Zoologists don't even know if it's there,
for it's never been seen at all.

U

The **Vino Bug** from the South of France
hops around in a gay sort of frolic.
As it eats nothing else but fermented grapes,
it is a confirmed alcoholic.

V

The **Warren Gimp** digs holes with its snout;
the reason for this is quite hazy.
It serves no purpose,
it's quite worn out,
but no-one can say that it's lazy.

W

The **X-Igoo** says "T-whit, t-whoo,"
which really annoys the owl,
who opens its eyes
and says in surprise,
"I think that your language is foul."

X

The **Yesser Bear**
can be found anywhere;
it crawls around on its knees.
You can give it a whack
and it won't hit back,
for it tries very hard to please.

Y

FLAP! FLAP!

The **Zimmer Bird** flies upside down
on alternate nights.
The reason that it flies upside down
is because it can't stand heights.

Z

Hi Noah,

We have arrived safely on an island, and we have called it Gubbemania. Our ark broke up when landing. We intend to use it to build a library. ALL ANIMALS SHOULD LEARN TO READ.

Thanks for the timber. We shall call it NOAH'S ARK-IVES. Have you any books, which the bookworms haven't eaten? Please respect our privacy. Keep away! Books can be left on the northern beach. Please reply by return pigeon. Thank you.

Arthur Gubbem

To: Captain Noah
The Ark
Mount Arrarat
1LFA FLUD

Printed in Great Britain
by Amazon